WRITTEN BY JENNIFER HOLDER

ILLUSTRATED BY KATHY PARKS

based on Matthew 4; John 6, 20, 21; Acts 2, 3, 5

Published by Standard Publishing, Cincinnati, Ohio
www.standardpub.com

ISBN 978-0-7847-2291-6

16 15 14 13 12 11 10 09   1 2 3 4 5

Standard®
PUBLISHING
Bringing The Word to Life

Cincinnati, Ohio

Peter loved to fish. One
day Jesus said to Peter,
"Come, follow me."

So Peter left his fishing boat and
became a disciple, or follower, of Jesus.
Peter and the other disciples traveled
with Jesus as he taught and helped and
loved the people.

Peter saw Jesus do great things only Jesus could do.
Peter was there when Jesus fed 5,000 men with just five
loaves and two fish.

Peter was there when Jesus walked on the water of a stormy lake.

Peter was with Jesus before Jesus died.

And three days later, Peter and John saw an empty tomb. Jesus had risen from the dead!

A few days later, Jesus asked Peter, "Do you love me?"
Peter said yes!

Then Jesus said, "Feed my lambs." Peter knew that when Jesus said "my lambs," he was talking about people who needed to know and follow Jesus. Peter needed to obey and tell others about Jesus.

So Peter went to Jerusalem and preached to a great crowd of all kinds of people.

Peter said, "Everyone who follows Jesus will be saved."

Peter went to the temple in Jerusalem too. He helped a man who could not walk, and he told even more people about Jesus. Peter preached, "Stop doing wrong. Turn to God."

More and more people wanted to hear about Jesus.
But some of the leaders became angry. They told Peter
and the other disciples to stop talking about Jesus. The
leaders even put Peter and the other disciples in jail!

But during the night, an angel from God opened the jail doors. The angel told the disciples to go tell about Jesus. And they did!

The leaders were angry again, but Peter said, "We must obey God." Peter kept telling people about Jesus. Many people listened to Peter. They wanted to follow Jesus.

Peter taught the people more about Jesus. The people learned to pray, to love one another, and to praise God.

Jesus asked Peter, "Do you love me?"
And Peter said yes!